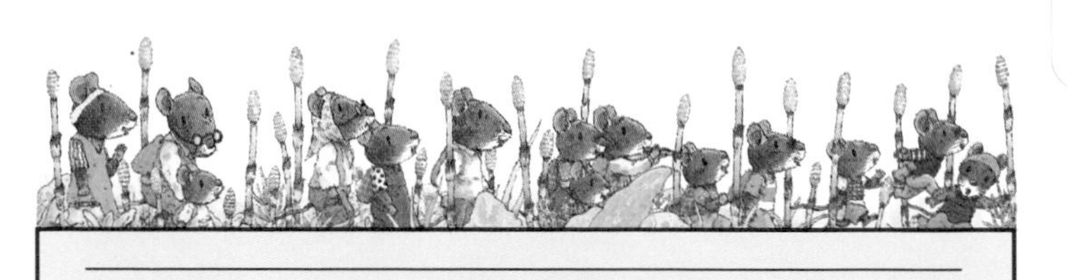

THE 14 FOREST MICE

and the

SUMMER LAUNDRY DAY

By Kazuo Iwamura

English text by MaryLee Knowlton

Gareth Stevens Children's Books
MILWAUKEE

For many days it had been hot and still in the forest. The summer sun beat down on

the Woodmouse family as they went about their chores.

But Mama had welcome news: “Gather your laundry, children!” she called. “It’s washing day!” The whole family got to work.

Laundry flew through the air and landed in strange places — sheets on heads, shirts on ears. “Do these things go too?” asked Daisy.

The first crew set off for the mountain stream. Everyone carried something. Grandpa, Papa, and Cashew stayed behind to finish their

chores. "We'll be along later," said Grandpa as he mopped his brow.

Mama stopped to smell the nodding lilies.
“Let’s hurry!” urged the little Woodmice.
“We have work to do!”

Mama just smiled. She knew why they were in such a hurry.

At last they arrived at the banks of a rushing mountain stream. Here, a breeze off the water was fresh and cool.

Insects whirred above their heads and chirped from the shade of the leaves.

Mama and her washing crew cooled off in the stream while they waited for Grandma and

the others. How refreshing it felt after the long, hot walk!

Dunk, dunk! Stomp, stomp! Rub, rub! Everyone had a job to do. Even little Iris washed her dolly's clothes.

Daisy hummed a tune under her breath as she danced a jig upon her favorite shirt.

Washing the sheets was a four-mouse job.
Wringing them out took two. Grandma was

finished with her washboard, so Cashew gave his new friend Froggie a ride.

The washing team was done, just in time for a game of flop-the-fish. Papa and Grandpa arrived with the wash poles — time to hang the

laundry to dry. “Look out!” cried Grandma. The washboard was drifting out of reach — and with Froggie aboard!

The swiftly moving mountain stream floated Froggie toward the waterfall! Hickory,

Chestnut, and Pecan dashed off in pursuit.
"Jump, Froggie! Jump!" they called out.

“Got it!” shouted Hickory. Froggie was safe — and so was the washboard!

Now for a swim! Cashew rode the waterfall down to where Pecan waited to grab him.

Papa and Grandpa had put up the drying poles. "Come on up!" they called over.

“We’ll dry the laundry in the breezy treetops.”
Six very clean mice climbed out of the stream.

High in the tree, the laundry flapped in the breeze. Soon everything would be dry —

except Cashew's shorts, which were headed back down to the stream!

The Woodmouse family relaxed while the breeze did its work. Some swung in hammocks made from clean sheets. Others enjoyed the

view from their lofty perch. Little pants, little shirts, pajamas, and sheets — everything clean!

With the laundry clean and dry, the Woodmice were ready to go home. But first, back to the

mountain stream — and good-bye to Froggie until next washing day.

For a free color catalog describing Gareth Stevens' list of high-quality books, call 1-800-542-2595 (USA) or 1-800-461-9120 (Canada). Gareth Stevens' Fax: (414) 225-0377.

THE 14 FOREST MICE
THE 14 FOREST MICE and the SPRING MEADOW PICNIC
THE 14 FOREST MICE and the SUMMER LAUNDRY DAY
THE 14 FOREST MICE and the HARVEST MOON WATCH
THE 14 FOREST MICE and the WINTER SLEDDING DAY

Library of Congress Cataloging-in-Publication Data

Iwamura, Kazuo, 1939-
The fourteen forest mice and the summer laundry day / by Kazuo Iwamura ;
[English text, MaryLee Knowlton]. — North American ed.
p. cm. — (The Fourteen forest mice)
Summary: The Forest Mice experience both hard work and a lot of fun when
they tackle a load of dirty laundry.
ISBN 0-8368-0576-3 (lib.bdg.)
ISBN 0-8368-1147-X (trade)
[1. Mice—Fiction. 2. Laundry—Fiction.] I. Knowlton, MaryLee,
1946- . II. Title. III. Title: 14 forest mice and the summer laundry day.
IV. Series: Iwamura, Kazuo, 1939- Fourteen forest mice.
PZ7.I954Fof 1991 [E]—dc20 90-50705

North American edition first published in 1991 by
Gareth Stevens Publishing
1555 North RiverCenter Drive, Suite 201
Milwaukee, Wisconsin 53212, USA

Design: Kristi Ludwig

Printed in the United States of America

2 3 4 5 6 7 8 9 99 98 97 96 95 94